PONIES *of Mykillengi*

PONIES
of Mykillengi

BY LONZO ANDERSON

ILLUSTRATED BY ADRIENNE ADAMS

CHARLES SCRIBNER'S SONS   New York

For Roger & Carol Henson,
who had their faces watched.

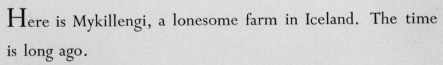

Here is Mykillengi, a lonesome farm in Iceland. The time
is long ago.

Winter. The farm lies still beneath the snow. The top
windows of the farmhouse peep like three eyes from under
the white cover.

Inside lives the family with the dog Yafti, the cows and eider ducks, all cozy and warm.

Father, Mother and Grandmother do their little winter work and wait for spring.

Rauf and Egli, the children, study while they wait. They go to school at home. Mother is the teacher.

The ponies, coated with winter fur, have a shelter open to the south, closed off from the cold north wind. There they wait out the winter storms, munching the dried fish-heads the children have given them because the last of the hay is gone.

Rauf's pony is named Jokull—"glacier"—because his mane and tail are as white as the glacier's ice.

Egli's pony is named Hekla, for the volcano that stands out there beyond the valley, beyond the hills. Hekla is a sunset roan with a mane that looks like fire when she rears and dances, and a tail like a river of red lava.

Hekla is beginning to feel fat and clumsy, for she is due to foal this spring.

The days are growing longer. Soon spring will come.

At last the warm wind blows from the south. Tufts of last year's grass show brown here and there in the melting snow. The ponies gallop in the meadow and stop to nibble at whatever they can find to eat.

The children watch them and cannot keep still.

"Please, Father," Rauf says, "may we ride over to the river to see if the salmon are running?"

"Yes," Father says. "But keep at a walk. Hekla is close to her time to foal, and you must not make her run."

"We promise!"

Off they go, over the low hill, through the mushy melting snow, toward the river.

At first the sun is bright, but before the children reach the river the sky grows dark. The south wind has stopped.

Cold is spreading slowly, silently over the land. Rauf and Egli shiver and button up tight.

Egli sighs. "Don't tell me it's going to snow again!"

"Looks that way," Rauf says, disappointed. "We'd better turn back."

Rauf heads Jokull for home. Egli turns Hekla to follow.

The world seems empty. No tree or fence, no road or living thing can the children see in any direction. The next farm is miles and miles away.

Suddenly the earth trembles and rumbles.

Rauf shouts, "Earthquake!"

The ponies' heads jerk high and their ears point. Their eyes roll, white around the edges. They are young and have never heard or felt an earthquake before, although in Iceland such things often happen.

Another jolt shakes the ground, harder this time, making the ponies stumble. The earth sways and shudders. The children hold tight, gasping.

Now with a wild roar the ground splits, making a big crack across the valley and hills.

The ponies fall to their knees and hocks, whinnying with fear. Egli screams and Rauf grunts in fright.

The roaring and shaking finally stop. In the silence the children hear only the frightened breathing of the ponies and the beating of their own hearts.

The crack in the earth lies between them and home. It is wide, and runs farther than they can see to the north and to the south. A vapor rises out of it.

The children crawl off the ponies to let them get to their feet. Cautiously they go to the edge of the rift. The fumes make them cough and sneeze, and they run back to the ponies.

Egli is scared. "What'll we *do*?"

"I wish I knew," Rauf says, breathing hard.

"Can we jump it with the ponies?"

Rauf studies the rift.

"Jokull could make it, I think," he says. "But Hekla, never—not in her condition."

The north wind is starting to whisper, and from the black clouds come drifting, sifting gently a few flakes of snow.

"A blizzard," Rauf says grimly. "That's the way it begins." This is just how it all happened before, when Father was a boy, with earthquake and snow and everything coming at once. He glances nervously at the big volcano in the distance. "Let's get moving!"

"But where *to?*" Egli is close to tears.

The north wind is growing stronger, colder.

"Well, not against the wind," Rauf says. "We'll go south. Maybe we can find the end of this thing, or a place to cross it."

Quickly they mount their ponies. Rauf leads the way southward along the rift. The volcano stands to the east, not yet hidden behind the falling snow.

Harder blows the wind, whistling out of the cold north. It spreads the thick, soft hairs at the top of each pony's tail. The hairs mat with snow and ice, making a shield that helps to protect against the wind's biting cold.

Hekla walks with her head hanging low. She stops, making soft grunting sounds in her throat. She is feeling a little sick. The fear and the falling have made the foal inside her stir and push and kick. She feels her body start to get ready to give birth to the little one. Because her body is preparing itself, the fear goes away.

Egli says, "Rauf, I mustn't ride her any more."

"You're right. I think the scare is going to make her have the foal a little early."

"Poor Hekla!"

"Ah, she'll be all right," Rauf says gruffly. "She's healthy, and she knows what to do. Here, you ride Jokull. I'll walk. We mustn't stop if we can help it."

Egli obeys him. Rauf takes Hekla's reins and leads her. Now it is night.

The wind makes the snowflakes fly like birds.

Egli shivers. "Rauf, I'm cold. I'd rather walk."

"Down you come, then."

They walk together. The ponies follow silently through the storm.

Hekla keeps slowing down. The muscles surrounding the foal within her are squeezing and rippling now, strongly

nudging and urging the little one toward the outside world. All by themselves the marvelous muscles work, without Hekla's making the slightest effort, and the foal is doing its part by struggling toward its birth.

Hekla knows that she cannot go any farther now. The time has come to be still.

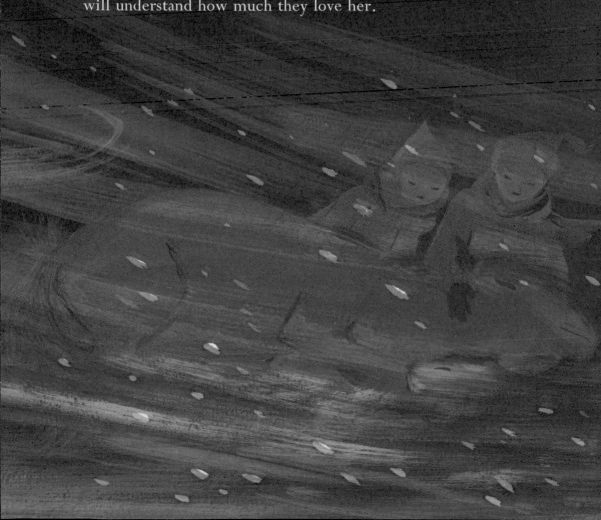

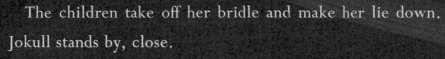

The children take off her bridle and make her lie down. Jokull stands by, close.

There in the snow, in the gray darkness, Hekla lets nature bring forth her foal. The muscles within her twitch, and relax, twitch, and relax. It is like the beating of her heart, but much stronger, slower—deeply exciting and satisfying.

Rauf is holding Hekla's head, not knowing what else to do. Both children caress her and whisper in her ear, hoping she will understand how much they love her.

Quickly and simply the foal is born. It has found its way out into the open air. It lies wet and glistening in the snow, moving its long legs uncertainly. It has burst out of the protecting sack in which it came. It starts to breathe.

Rauf and Egli watch silently, their eyes wide with wonder.

They want to pet the foal, but they know they must not touch it yet. It is Hekla's. She will clean and warm and love it.

The children huddle there with the ponies. They worry about the family and home and what harm the earthquake may have done. They worry about Hekla and her foal and how to get them safely back to Mykillengi.

The foal is a restless little thing, wanting to learn to stand. It keeps struggling up and flopping down, making funny gasping sounds, eagerly breathing the cold clean air of the Iceland world.

At last, all wobbly in the knees, it stands.

Hekla is on her feet now. She nuzzles the foal close, to warm it and let it drink her milk.

The blackness in the sky and the white snow lashing at the earth make a wild gray world.

"Dark as the inside of a white cow," Rauf says. This is an old joke they have heard from Father, and it makes them smile in spite of their troubles.

Suddenly the rumbling sounds start again, but this time they come from the volcano, miles away.

"Just as Father said, remember?" Rauf shivers as he speaks. "The earthquake, the storm, then the volcano. They go together."

Egli moves closer to her brother, her eyes big with fear.

Now comes a tremendous roar. The mountain seems on fire. Its top is a mass of flame and smoke. Streams of melted rock flow down its sides like molasses. The brightness shows even through the snowstorm.

The night is like a dull-red day. The earth seems to shake on its foundation.

Jokull and Hekla shelter the foal between them. It can
now stand steady on its feet. It nuzzles up beneath its mother
and drinks her warm milk even as she trembles with fear.

The children cling together, too scared to think.

But a strange and wonderful thing happens. The explosion of the volcano shakes loose a mass of rock and mud from the hillside that tumbles into the rift and fills a part of it.

Now there is a way across. They can go home!

The rubble of the landslide makes rough going. The children pick up the foal between them and carry it. Its legs are so long and wiggly that they have a lot of trouble, but finally they manage to get across, with Hekla worrying and fretting behind them, and Jokull in the rear.

The light from the volcano is dimmer now, but the children and ponies know the way, even in the dark. Back along the rift they walk toward home.

The storm is slowing now. The snow is not so blinding.

Far ahead shines a swinging lantern. Egli sees it first. Father's legs cast long, twinkling shadows in its light as he rushes along the rift, looking for the lost ones. Yafti, the dog, makes his own bouncing shadow.

"Father, Father!" Egli cries. "Here we are!"

Rauf yells, "Over here!"

The lantern swings up and down and sideways, signaling.

Yafti begins to bark. Father's voice, so far away it sounds
like a whisper across the snow, says, "I'm coming!"

Yafti reaches them first, barking and leaping up and licking the children's faces.

Father comes panting and gathers them in his big arms.

"How's it at home? Mama? Grandma?" the children ask in one breath.

"Fine, fine," Father says. "A few cracks in the house— can be fixed. I'd have found you sooner, but I went the wrong way along the rift at first. Come. Home we go!"

He puts both children on Jokull's back. "It's all right. He's strong. Let Hekla take it easy."

The foal is exhausted now. Father picks it up and carries it. It is too tired to struggle. Its long legs dangle like ropes.

The little parade pushes homeward through the snow. Father leads the way, and Hekla follows closely, to stay near her foal. Jokull is next, with two worn-out children on his back, and Yafti comes along behind.

The lights of the farmhouse show ahead. Mykillengi—
home at last!

Mother comes through the lighted doorway, holding out
her arms in welcome. Grandma is close behind.

All the family is together again. Hot food is on the table.

The volcano still grumbles and glows in the distance, but that will not last, Father is sure, for he has seen it all before.

Rauf and Egli eat their late supper, smiling sleepily. Soon they will be safe in bed.

Jokull and Hekla are calmly munching their food once more in the shelter, and the foal is sucking its mother's warm milk.

The snow will melt again, and the grass come green.

The foal will grow and learn to eat the grass and answer when the children call.